A Family That Fights

Sharon Chesler Bernstein

Illustrated by **Karen Ritz**

ALBERT WHITMAN & COMPANY • Morton Grove, Illinois

To the children who shared their stories with me. S.C.B.
To Pat, Lori, and Ryan. K.R.

The illustrations are pencil.
The text typeface is Stone Informal.
Designed by Karen Johnson Campbell.

Library of Congress Cataloging-in-Publication Data
Bernstein, Sharon Chesler.
A family that fights/Sharon Chesler Bernstein;
pictures by Karen Ritz.
p.   cm.
Summary: Henry's parents fight often and his
father sometimes hits his mother, causing Henry to
feel frightened and ashamed. Includes a list of
things children can do in situations of
family violence.
ISBN 0-8075-2248-1
[1. Family violence—Fiction. 2. Family problems—
Fiction.] I. Ritz, Karen, ill. II. Title.
PZ7.B457Fam   1991   90-29889
[Fic]—dc20   CIP
                                       AC

Domestic violence is a strong subject for a children's book, but there is nothing shown here that a child in a violent family has not already seen. There is no feeling reflected that the child has not felt.

Ideally, a caring adult should share *A Family That Fights* with a child or a group of children. (I include parents who hit each other in the category of caring adult.) If you are a parent who beats or has been beaten, this book can help you talk to your children about how it feels to live with family violence. If you are an adult involved with children professionally, you can use the book in much the same way.

It is very difficult to explain adult behavior. Instead, try to help the child express his or her own tangled feelings about the fighting at home. While at first a child may be reluctant to discuss family violence, he or she eventually will be relieved and reassured that you are willing to talk and, most of all, to listen.

All families get along sometimes and disagree sometimes. When they disagree, people in some families argue in firm, quiet voices. Some people holler and scream at each other. But people in other families fight with hands and fists, or with sticks and other weapons that hurt.

Claire, Joe, and Henry live in a family that goes to movies, bakes cookies, plays games, and builds snowmen. It is also a family where the dad fights with his hands.

Claire is six, and she is quiet. She plays a lot by herself. She loves her dollhouse. Sometimes her doll family has fights like her mom and dad do. Sometimes the daddy hits the mommy. One time the girl doll, Emily, ran away. But she had to come back because she had nowhere else to go.

Henry is the bigger boy. He is eight. Sometimes he pretends that nothing is wrong with his family. But mostly he worries. He knows adults are not supposed to hit each other. He is afraid that his mother will be badly hurt, and that neighbors or kids at school will find out his father hits his mother.

Henry also worries about Claire and about Joe, who is only three. He knows they get scared when Dad yells real loud and hits Mom.

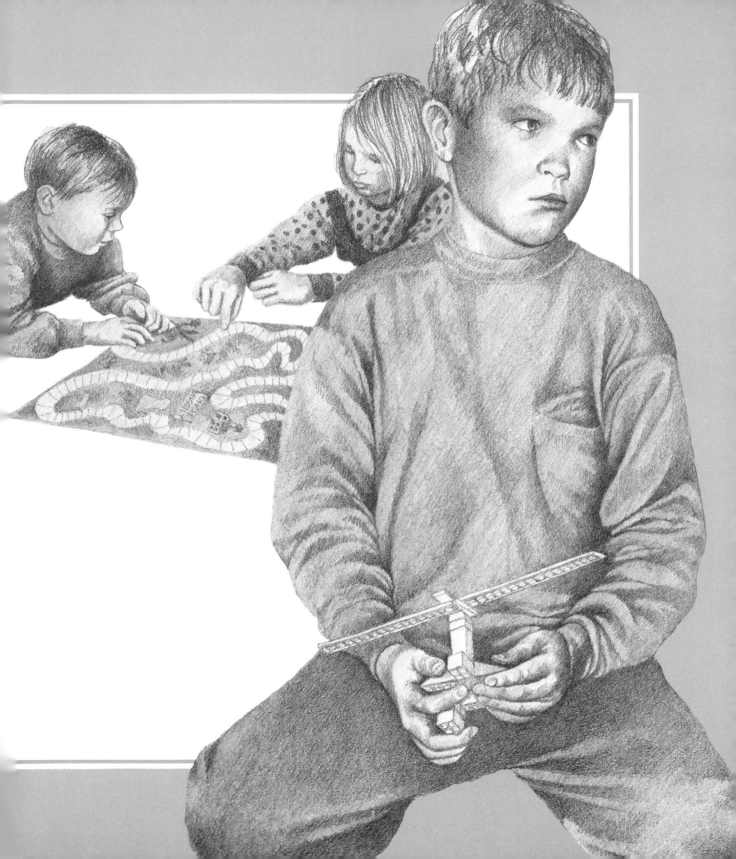

The worst time of day is when Dad comes home. Henry can tell that his mom gets real nervous. Henry knows she is scared because Dad might be in a bad mood.

As soon as Dad comes home, everyone knows what kind of mood he's in. If he's feeling happy, he scoops Joe up and puts him on his shoulders. He laughs and tells silly riddles.

If he's in a bad mood, anything can start a fight. If Mom is late with dinner, Dad goes in the kitchen and slams pots and dishes around. Or he may say he doesn't like what she cooked. He sits at the table and says how bad the food is. Sometimes he grabs Mom by the arm and drags her into the kitchen, where he yells at her.

When Dad is in such a bad mood, Henry tries to make Claire and Joe be especially good. While Mom and Dad are fighting, he tries to get the little kids to finish all their food. Then no one will be mad at them, and Mom won't think she is a bad cook.

Often a fight begins at night. Henry buries his head in the pillow when the yelling and hitting start. He hopes that Joe will not wake up. If a fight wakes Joe, he cries so hard that Claire comes in crying, too.

Usually the three of them sit close together on Joe's bed. They can't see what is going on—they can only hear shouting and slamming. Once Claire wanted to go downstairs to stop Dad. Henry was afraid this would make things even worse. He told Claire to stay right there, but she got up anyway. Then Henry hit her to make her sit down. He didn't mean to—it just happened.

Henry was relieved because Claire listened to him after he hit her. She stayed upstairs. But he also worried because he hadn't thought about hitting Claire. He just did it. When Claire cried, Henry felt ashamed.

If Joe and Claire scream during the fighting, Dad comes in. Mom follows him. Dad shouts real loud. Sometimes he takes off his belt and hits it against the toy chest. Mom pulls on him and cries.

Henry is always afraid that Dad will hit him or Joe or Claire. Dad never has, but Henry is scared that someday he will.

Sometimes Mom is bleeding, and then Claire and Joe cry even harder. One time Joe ran up to Dad and screamed, "You stop hurting her!" Dad reached down to hit him, but Mom stepped between them, and Dad hit her instead.

When the fight is over, Dad usually leaves the house. Mom takes Claire to her room and tucks her in. Then she comes back to hold Joe and rock him to sleep. Henry lies in bed and thinks about what he will do to Dad when he grows up.

If Henry tries to talk to his mother, she says he shouldn't worry. She explains that Dad doesn't mean to hit her, and he always feels bad when he does. She doesn't seem to understand how scary the fights are. Henry feels angry when his mother pretends nothing is wrong.

He wishes he could tell someone about his family, but he never does. Henry feels ashamed, ashamed of his father. He feels ashamed to be a part of this family.

At school, Henry sometimes thinks about his father hitting his mother. One day, when he was supposed to be doing dictionary work, he drew a picture of a firing squad shooting a man. Mrs. Carlson called on him to answer a question, but he couldn't because he hadn't heard what she'd said. Mrs. Carlson was nice, but the kids all laughed. Now Henry doesn't draw in class anymore, but he stares out the window a lot and makes up pictures in his head.

Henry knows that other families are not like his. When he stays over at his friend Nick's house, he sometimes hears Nick's parents argue, but no one gets real mad. Soon he hears them laughing about something.

Once he and Nick spilled a whole bowl of popcorn on the living room couch. They had been trying to see who could get the most popcorn into his hand at once.

Nick's father just rolled his eyes and said, "You guys better clean that up right away." He got the vacuum out, and Nick and Henry cleaned up the mess.

That night, when he slept over at Nick's house, Henry pretended he lived there.

But Dad can be fun lots of times. In the summer, he's helped Nick and Henry set up a little tent in the yard so they can sleep out. Sometimes, if the kids all ask, Dad gets out his silly hats and tells a story about where he bought each one.

Claire and Joe and Mom like to play cards, and when they do, Henry and his father play checkers or computer games. When the games are finished, Dad makes a big pot of hot cocoa—from scratch, not from packets. Henry's mom says his dad makes the best cocoa in the world.

Henry wishes his family could always have fun like this. He always hopes that his dad will never get angry again. But he thinks that probably his dad will hit his mother again sometime, and that he and Claire and Joe cannot stop him.

Even though Henry's father is a grown-up, he has not learned to express his angry feelings in a grown-up way. Instead, when he is upset or frustrated, he acts mean. He shouts and bullies and hits. Adults who lose control like this still have more growing up to do.

Henry, Claire, and Joe need to talk about how scared and sad they feel when Dad hits Mom. They must remember *they are not to blame,* even if Dad says they are. Even if they sometimes make mistakes, they are not the reason their dad hits their mom.

Henry, Claire, and Joe are good children who live in a family with a very difficult problem.

Claire, Joe, and Henry cannot stop the fighting in their home, no matter how good they are. But they can try to do things to help themselves.

1. They can talk to their parents, when there is no fighting, about how awful it feels when their dad hits their mom.

2. They can plan with their parents to have a "safe" house or place where they can go when their parents are fighting.

3. They can ask their mom and dad to see a family helper like a counselor, doctor, nurse, minister, or teacher.

4. They can tell a grandparent, aunt or uncle, a grown-up friend, a friend's parents, or a family helper how they feel when their parents fight.

5. They can draw pictures of what they are feeling.

6. They can do things that make them happy like reading favorite books, playing games, watching TV shows, and talking to friends on the phone or visiting them.

7. They can try to understand that they are not the reason their father hits their mother.

Here are some things that parents can do in a family where the father hits the mother.

1. The father can talk to a special helper like a counselor or therapist. Some grown-up men who cannot control their anger also meet, with a counselor, in groups with other men who have this problem.

2. The mother can get help from a therapist or counselor.

3. She can call 911—the police number—if she feels she is in danger.

4. She can call a national hotline number for domestic violence. The number is 1-800-333-SAFE. It answers 24 hours a day, and the people there will provide immediate help (the police or an ambulance) or tell the caller other ways she can help herself.

5. She can call a local hotline number for domestic violence. The telephone operator can provide this number.

6. She and the children can stay for a while with a friend or relative, or at a shelter for women whose husbands hit them.